W9-BPJ-715

MICHELLE ANTHONY

Illustrated by Cory Godbey

THE BIG GOD STORY
Published by David C. Cook
4050 Lee Vance View
Colorado Springs, CO 80918 U.S.A.

David C. Cook Distribution Canada
55 Woodslee Avenue, Paris, Ontario, Canada N3L 3E5

David C. Cook U.K., Kingsway Communications
Eastbourne, East Sussex BN23 6NT, England

LCCN 2010925761
ISBN 978-1-4347-6454-6
eISBN 978-1-4347-0240-1

The Team: Don Pape, Kate Etue, Amy Kiechlin, Caitlyn York, Karen Athen
Cover and interior illustrations: Cory Godbey

Printed in China
First Edition 2010

1 2 3 4 5 6 7 8 9 10

041910

This Book Belongs To:

____

This is not just any story. It is a true story, full of mysterious people and secret plans and last-second escapes. It's God's Big Story, and every part tells us about His promise to love us. But let's not get ahead of ourselves. Let's start at the very beginning, when God made the world …

A long, long time ago, God created a beautiful garden called Eden. Chatty birds built nests in colorful fruit trees, and playful puppies romped in the soft grass. It was Adam and Eve's home. God made them, too, and they were His friends. But Adam and Eve chose to disobey God, and this ruined their friendship with Him. But God didn't forget them. He made a promise that was going to make things better!

The promise was that God would send a Redeemer to take away this punishment so that people could be friends with Him again, this time … forever!

Adam and Eve weren't the only ones who disobeyed God. Eventually, everyone on earth had made so many bad choices that God decided the world needed a fresh start.

But Noah loved God. He was the only man on earth who did, so God had a plan to keep Noah's family safe. It involved lots of wood, a huge boat, thousands of animals, and few strange looks from curious neighbors.

God's plan worked! The flood came, but Noah and his family were safe in the ark as the rain washed away the world and everything in it. When the rain dried up, Noah and his family thanked God for rescuing them. But their real rescue was still to come … so they waited for the promise.

Years later, dads told the story of the great flood around campfires. But there was a very old man named Abraham who had no children to tell this story to.

But God had a plan for Abraham. Even though Abraham and his wife were very old, God promised He would give them more children than there are stars in the sky, more kids than there is sand on the beach! His family would be God's people.

The promise was hard to believe, but Abraham and Sarah trusted God's promise … and He gave them a baby boy named Isaac! God kept His promise to give them a son, and He was going to keep His promise to send a Redeemer, too!

Isaac had a grandson named Joseph. Joseph was a good boy, but he had mean brothers. Sometimes brothers fight, but Joseph's brothers were mean and selfish, so they sent him away! They tricked Joseph and sold him to be a slave in a faraway place called Egypt.

Even though Joseph was sad to be all alone in a strange place and missed his family, he trusted that God would take care of him. And God did. Years later, Joseph was able to forgive his brothers and take care of them, too.

Joseph's family built homes and had babies, and eventually thousands of God's people lived in Egypt. But they were slaves, and they spent long days in the hot sun doing hard work. They had tired backs and sad hearts, and they cried out for God to rescue them.

God chose a man named Moses to tell Pharaoh to let His people go free. But Pharaoh said no. So God sent terrible plagues, and finally Pharaoh told Moses to take his people and leave Egypt for good! They escaped in the night to make the long journey to the Promised Land, their new home.

“Are we there yet?” the Israelites asked. They had no idea how long their trip would really take! They started to doubt at every detour and complain at every crossroad. They ended up wandering in the desert for forty years!

When they finally got to the Promised Land, they were surprised to find huge giants and dangerous men living there. Many people were scared, but not Joshua. He was a warrior who believed God wanted them to live in this place. So he pulled out his sword and bravely led the people of God into the Promised Land!

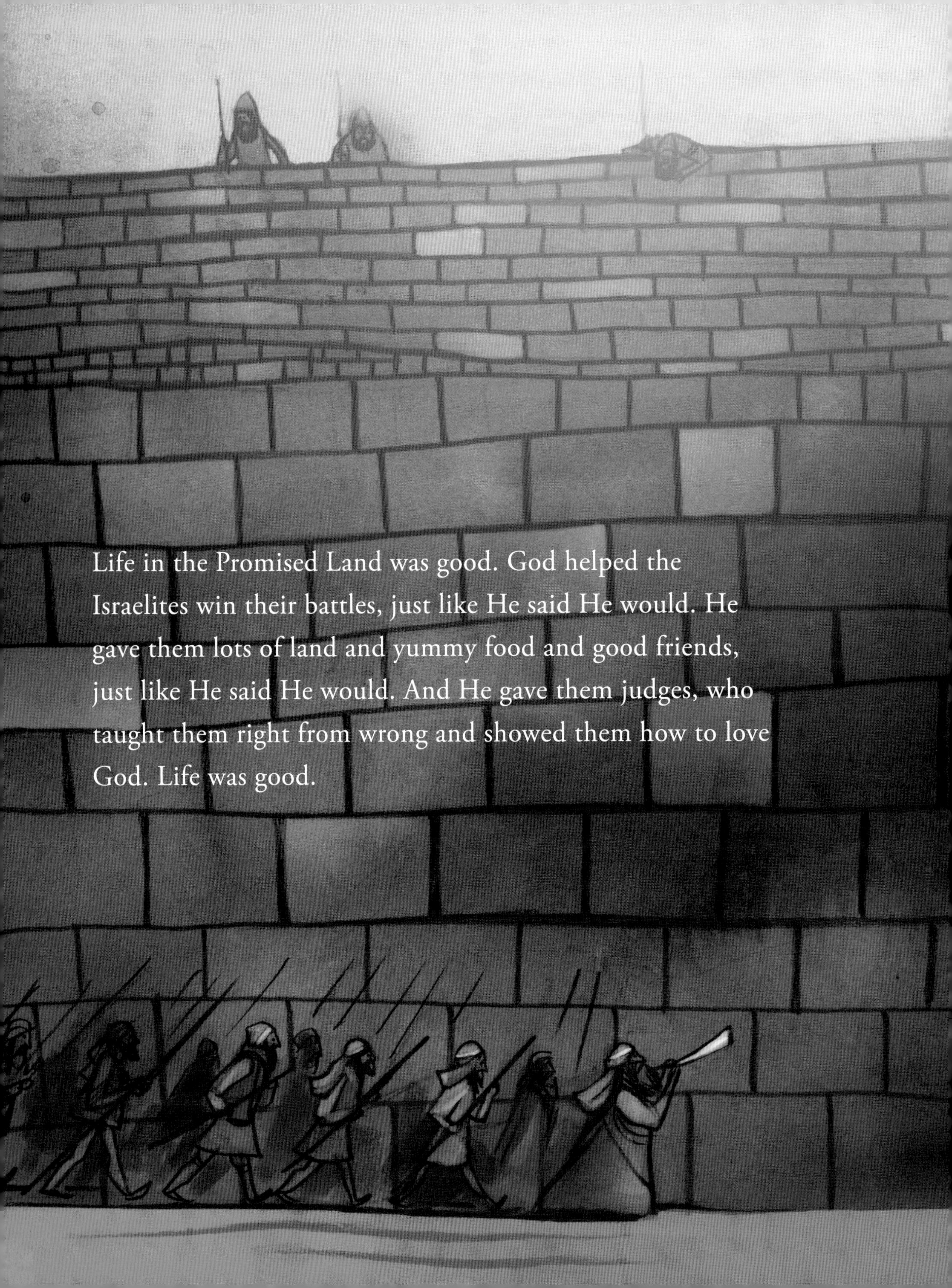

Life in the Promised Land was good. God helped the Israelites win their battles, just like He said He would. He gave them lots of land and yummy food and good friends, just like He said He would. And He gave them judges, who taught them right from wrong and showed them how to love God. Life was good.

But the Israelites weren't happy being different. When they saw that other people had kings, they wanted a king too. They whined and complained and stomped their feet and waved their fists until the judges reminded them that God was their king. He'd done everything He said He would. He always kept His promises. What more could they want?

The Israelites wouldn't listen. All they thought about was what they wanted.

So they chose Saul to be their king. He was tall and good-looking. Little boys wanted to fight like him, and little girls wanted to be princesses in his palace. But Saul wasn't a good king. He didn't listen to God, and Israel was in trouble.

God had to step in and fix the mess they'd made. He chose David, a shepherd boy, to be Israel's next king. No one would have expected it, but he was the strong and mighty king Israel had hoped for. Why? Because he loved God.

Eventually Jerusalem was destroyed, and God's people lived in faraway lands. In one of these places, the king's men tried to tell Daniel and his friends who they could pray to and what they could eat, but they obeyed God instead of these silly rules.

The king's men became so angry with Daniel and his friends that they locked Daniel in a cave with lions and pushed his friends into a fiery oven. But God protected them, and Daniel and his friends lived to tell everyone that God always keeps His promises!

Esther was very poor. She was an orphan. She had nothing at all. Nothing, that is, except God's promise and His plan: Esther would one day be the queen of Persia.

But life as a queen wasn't all pastries and parties! God had a job for Esther. His people, the Jews, were in danger, and Esther would have to risk everything to save them.

So one night, during a great feast, she put on her prettiest dress and her most sparkly jewelry and went to see the king. She told him the truth about the plot to hurt God's people. It was scary, but Esther obeyed God, and the Jews were saved!

The Jews went back to their homes in Jerusalem, but when they got there, they were very sad. It was an old and war-ruined city. So God gave Nehemiah the job of building new walls for His city.

Nehemiah didn't have big yellow bulldozers or shiny silver tools, but he did have God's power on his side. Many people made fun of him and tried to ruin the work he was doing, but Nehemiah didn't give up! He finished the wall, and now the new city would be safe.

But then something strange happened

God was silent for a long time

Nearly four hundred years passed without a word from God. Just silence. But even though God was quiet, He wasn't gone. His promise was still alive; it was just hidden.

Then, on a dark night in a dusty stable on the edges of the town of Bethlehem, God's promise to His people came true. Jesus was born! Joseph and Mary held their little baby, the child of God, as shepherds and angels sang His glory.

Jesus grew up in Nazareth and studied God's Word like the other boys His age, but it was clear that Jesus was not an ordinary boy—He was God, the Promise, the Redeemer for all people.

When He grew up, Jesus chose twelve friends to help Him teach people about God's love. These disciples helped the poor, healed the sick, and were friends to lonely people. Jesus taught the world a new way to live—God's way. Many people believed the good news He taught—that one day soon they could be friends with God again!

It was time for God's plan to take place. Soldiers came and took Jesus away in the dark of night. You see, in order to be our Redeemer, Jesus had to die. That was the only way we could be friends with God again. But that's not the end of this Big Story.

Jesus didn't stay dead—three days later, an angel rolled back the heavy stone door to His tomb, and it was empty! Jesus was alive again, proving to all people that He was Christ, the Lord!

One day Jesus will return to earth again, and everyone in the whole world will know that He is the strong and mighty King of Kings!

Those who love God and believe in the promise of the Redeemer will live with Him in a new heaven and new earth. We'll be perfect friends with Him, just like it was in the garden in the beginning. The way it should be … forever and ever!

You've just read the Big God Story, but it's not The End! You can be part of the Big God Story too and tell others about God's great promise.

I want to be part of the Big God Story too!

____

Dear Reader,

There is no greater privilege than to teach a child the story of God's great love. Although the truths of the Bible are so magnificent and endless that we continue to learn and discover them our entire lives, they are also simple enough for children of any age to understand as well—that's the beauty of His story!

On each page of *The Big God Story*, children will see that God promised, preserved, prophesied, and faithfully presented His Redeemer at the perfect time! What's so important for your child—and us—to learn is that He wasn't just rescuing us, He was redeeming us, getting us back into a right relationship with God. But, as you can imagine, I couldn't cover everything I wanted to in the space of thirty-six pages. So the publisher worked with me to create an online forum where you can access expanded content, child-friendly definitions of theological terms, conversation starters for you and your child, and more! This will enhance the role you play in the spiritual nurturing of a young child. Visit http://davidccook.com/BigGodStory to access this wonderful material.

Remember, God's story is still being written, and you and I can be a part of it. Today, as we receive Jesus the Redeemer, the promise continues in each one of us. May God bless you as you train young hearts to glorify Him with their lives!

In Him,
Michelle Anthony